The Magic Mirror

Riya,
Love your elders,
love yourself!

Zetta Elliott

The Magic Mirror

Illustrations by Paul Melecky

Rosetta
&
Press

Books by Zetta Elliott

A Wish After Midnight
Bird
Max Loves Muñecas!
Room in My Heart
Ship of Souls
The Boy in the Bubble
The Deep
The Girl Who Swallowed the Sun
The Phoenix on Barkley Street

"You're awfully quiet, Kamara. Did something happen at school today?"

I shake my head and pretend to look out the car window. If I think about Malik Patterson and his nasty words, I might start to cry all over again.

It's Tuesday and that means it's time to visit the big, old house where my grandmother lives. Last year Gramma had a stroke. Mama says her mother is too proud to ask for help, so once a week we bring dinner over so that Gramma doesn't have to cook. Mama and I also make sure that the house is clean and tidy. We do the laundry, sweep the porch, and rake up leaves in the yard. We do all the things Gramma can no longer do by herself.

I don't mind doing the extra chores. I'd do anything for my grandmother. Since the stroke it's hard for Gramma to get around, even with her cane. But Gramma hasn't changed inside. When she wraps me in her arms and holds me close to her warm, soft body, I feel like I'm in the safest place on earth—a place where boys like Malik Patterson can't reach me with their horrible, hurtful words.

When we arrive, Gramma is standing on the porch waiting for us. I can't wait to feel safe in her arms. I run toward the house and bury my face in Gramma's flowery apron. I wrap my arms around her waist and feel Gramma squeezing me tight. I don't want to cry again, but two hot tears slide down my cheeks just the same.

Gramma asks, "How's my beautiful girl?"

I try to answer but instead I choke on the lump of pain in my throat.

Gramma tips my face up and looks at me. "What's the matter, baby?"

I can't say anything because I'm really crying now. Mama says she'll be in the kitchen. Gramma pulls me onto the porch swing. She puts her arm around me and uses her cane to start us rocking. After a while, I start to feel quiet inside.

I tell Gramma about what happened at school today. She listens patiently and shakes her head.

"Those are some hard words," says Gramma as she passes me her handkerchief. "Words like those can tear a hole in your soul."

I blow my nose and nod quietly. I knew Gramma would understand.

Mama comes up to the screen door and tells us that dinner is ready. Gramma uses her cane to stop the swing from rocking.

"Not yet," she says to Mama. "First there's something I need Kamara to do for me."

I slide off the swing and wait for my grandmother to tell me what to do. She smiles at me but I see that her eyes are almost as sad as mine. Gramma cradles my face with her soft, worn palm.

"Kamara, I need you to go upstairs to the guest room. There's an old mirror in there." Gramma pauses and looks at me, hard. "Make sure you give it a good scrubbing, you hear?"

"Yes, Gramma," I say before going into the kitchen to get a rag and some cleanser. Then I head upstairs.

My grandmother's house is more than a hundred years old. The floors creak when you walk on them, and shadows whisper down the long, dark halls. Since her stroke, Gramma doesn't come upstairs any more. She doesn't have many visitors either, so the guest room hardly ever gets used. It's at the end of the hallway. Like all the other rooms on the second floor, the door to the guest room is closed. I turn the glass doorknob and go inside.

The room is quiet and still. Faint rays of sunshine squeeze through the closed shutters. The air is stale and thick with dust.

All the furniture in the guest room is covered with white sheets, but I know which mirror Gramma wants me to clean. It stands in a far corner of the room. I go over and open the shutters. I lift the window a little bit to let in some fresh air. Then I pull the sheet off the mirror.

Like almost everything in my grandmother's house, this mirror is very old. It first belonged to Gramma's grandmother, Loretta Mae Williams. She gave it to her daughter, Janie Louise Ellerby, and she passed it on to Gramma. Gramma's full name is Mae Jean Heston. One day Gramma will give the mirror to her daughter, Loretta. And when I am grown up, Mama will give it to me, Kamara Louise.

Despite the sheet, the mirror is still covered with dust. I spray cleanser on my rag and begin to scrub the glass. When I am done, the mirror shines as if it were brand new.

I stand back and stare at my reflection. I look at my lips, my eyes, my nose, and my hair. I touch my cheek and wonder if the mean things Malik said are true. Gramma calls me beautiful, but that's because she loves me so much. I wonder what other people see when they look at me.

Suddenly a gust of wind blows through the open window. I shiver and look outside. A huge cloud passes in front of the sun. Behind me the door creaks eerily before clicking shut. Without any sunlight, the room is dark. I shiver again and look at Gramma's mirror.

For some reason I can barely see my reflection. The image is fuzzy and dark. I take my rag and begin to scrub the mirror once more. As I am scrubbing, something strange starts to happen. The wind blows harder, the room gets darker, and the mirror begins to glow!

I drop my rag and step back from the glowing mirror. I can no longer see my reflection. Instead I see a huge ship bobbing on a shimmering, black sea. The waves sparkle like diamonds beneath the full, white moon, but there is something ugly about this scene. I step closer to the mirror and hear the splash of oars dipping into water. Then I see a smaller boat approaching a tall ship.

There are four white sailors in the rowboat and six enslaved Africans. I know they have been enslaved because they have iron chains around their ankles, wrists, and necks. The Africans have delicate lines traced on their cheeks and they are whispering to each other in a language I do not know. The sailors look like pirates to me. They laugh cruelly and take turns drinking from a brown jug.

One of the slaves is a girl who looks about the same age as me. Her eyes are large and full of fear, but she is too proud to cry in front of her captors. She bites down on her lip instead.

When the rowboat reaches the ship, the Africans are forced to climb up onto the deck. The captain looks them over with a greedy eye. He does not ask their names. He simply chooses new names and writes them down in his book. Then a door is opened and the shivering Africans are taken below deck. Cries of despair rise into the starry night.

Before she is taken away, the African girl turns and looks at me. I can tell that she is frightened but she is trying to be brave. I see the courage shining in her eyes. I try to reach out and comfort her, but my fingers stop at the mirror's surface. The African girl nods at me and then disappears below deck.

I take my fingers away from the mirror. I cannot believe this is happening! I want to leave the guest room but my feet refuse to move. I want the sun to come out again but the sky is still dark with clouds.

I look at the glowing mirror. A new scene meets my eyes. A bright, hot sun shines in the blue sky. I see a field full of cotton. Black women, men, and children in shabby clothes are hunched over the prickly plants. At one end of the field, a white man on a horse watches them work. He hollers at them to hurry up. He has a whip in his hand.

I look closely at the slaves until I see a teenage girl who looks strangely familiar. She is pulling the white bolls off the cotton plants and stuffing them in a long sack that drags on the ground. Her fingers are bleeding and her back is sore. I can tell that she is tired. Suddenly she starts to sing.

> *Steal away, steal away,*
> *Steal away to Jesus.*
> *Steal away, steal away home;*
> *I ain't got long to stay here.*

Her voice is as clear and pure as cold water. The other slaves sigh as they listen to her, and then join in. They sing slowly, sorrowfully.

I watch the girl carefully. As she passes other young slaves working in the field she whispers to them, "Tonight's the night." The overseer cannot hear her because of the singing.

The girl looks at me and I can see the determination in her eyes. I think she is planning to run away. I wish that I could help her find her way to freedom, but she must get there on her own. She nods at me as if she understands, and then continues filling her sack with cotton.

Before I know what is happening, the scene in the mirror changes again. It is night. The inky sky is full of stars, but one star in particular shines especially bright. A small, wood cabin sits in a clearing. A single candle burns brightly in the window, and a star-patterned quilt hangs over the fence.

Inside the cabin a silver-haired woman is hiding runaway slaves in her secret cellar. She hears dogs barking in the distance and hurries to lay a rug over the trap door. The old woman is trembling. She takes a deep breath and says a quick prayer. Then she wraps herself in a shawl and goes outside.

Several white men on horseback have entered her yard. They have guns, and dogs, and torches that burn like fury in the night.

"We're looking for a group of runaways. You got company tonight?"

The old woman lifts her chin up high and calmly says, "No, sir."

One of the patrollers pushes past her and goes inside the cabin. He comes back out a moment later and shakes his head. "They ain't here."

The patrollers ride off into the night. The old woman gathers the quilt off the fence and goes back inside. She opens the trap door and tells the runaways it is safe to come out. She gives them each a bundle of food and tells them to follow the North Star to freedom.

"God bless you," they say before slipping into the night.

The old woman closes the door and sits down at her table. I watch her as she wraps herself tightly in her shawl. Although she is trembling, I know that she is brave. She must be a conductor on the Underground Railroad.

For a brief moment the old woman looks at me. Then she puts the candle back in the window and waits for more runaways to arrive.

The mirror changes scenes again. This time I hear children screaming and crying. I see a young teacher standing in a classroom surrounded by her terrified students. She is pressed against the wall next to the window. Outside men wearing white robes are standing next to a burning cross.

"We warned you!" yells one of the hooded men.

The teacher tells her students to run outside and hide in the woods. The children are frightened, but they do as they are told. Smoke begins to fill the tiny schoolhouse.

Though it is difficult to breathe, the teacher starts gathering books and papers in her arms. She rushes outside and throws everything on the ground. Then she takes a deep breath and goes back into the burning building.

My heart is pounding in my chest. I grip the frame of the mirror and wait for her to come back out. I hear someone coughing and hope that she is alive. A moment later, the teacher emerges carrying more books and a spinning globe. She collapses on the ground and is surrounded by her worried students.

The men in the white robes go away once they are

certain the building has been destroyed. Anxious parents arrive and search frantically for their children.

I look at the young teacher as she watches her schoolhouse burn. Her face is smeared with soot and tears. I know that she is angry. Yet when she presses her lips together, I can tell that she will not give up. She has managed to save her students, her books, and her teaching tools. She will open another school, and she will continue to teach her students in the evening once they have finished working in the fields.

The young teacher looks at me and nods. Then, with the help of her students, she begins gathering the books that lie scattered on the ground.

I step back from the mirror and try to catch my breath. So much has happened so quickly! When I am ready, I look into the mirror again.

I see a bustling city scene. The sidewalks overflow with a surging river of bodies. High above the street, a man blows into a golden trumpet and showers the concrete

with sound. Children play hopscotch and stickball on the shady side streets. Subway trains rumble underground. This is Harlem!

Harlemites have stories to tell. They paint, sing, dance, and sculpt. They use jazz, the blues, and the written word to make their stories come alive.

When migrants reach the city, they start to feel brand new. People who have always lived in the city sense that things are starting to change. This is a moment of rebirth. They call it a *renaissance*.

A young woman sits at a desk next to a window. She looks out over the busy Harlem street and smiles softly to herself. America is changing. Her people still face violence, poverty, and discrimination—even in cities like New York. But the young writer feels optimistic that things will not always be this way.

She looks at me and I can see hope lighting up her eyes. She takes her pen and writes:

> *We are the roots*
> *that will push*
> *this tree up*

through earth
rocky with prejudice…

The mirror dims, then glows bright again. I see a crowded pier. A ship's anchor is slowly being raised, and men in khaki uniforms are waving from the deck. These soldiers are heading off to war. Wives, mothers, sisters, and daughters stand on the pier calling out their good-byes. Some women cry into their handkerchiefs. Others stand on the pier, silent and still, long after the ship has sailed away.

The scene in the mirror changes. I hear the deafening sound of drills and hammers pounding against steel. A spray of orange sparks lights up a dark factory. Most of the men, white and black, have gone off to fight in the war. Workers are still needed, however, and so women take their place in the factories.

Some white women do not want to work with black women. They refuse to share their lockers, or to use

machines black women have touched. But America is at war, and the country can no longer afford to discriminate. Doors that were closed are slowly starting to open.

A welder turns off her blowtorch and raises her heavy facemask. She reminds me of my mama. The welder takes her glove off and wipes the sweat from her brow with the back of her hand. I can see how tired she is.

Workers must put in long hours to meet the demands of the war. But when this woman looks at me, I can see how proud she is. Proud to be helping her country. Proud to show others that she is capable and strong. Proud to be earning money that helps support her family.

Before she lowers her facemask again, the woman smiles at me. Then she turns her blowtorch back on, and blue sparks shower her like rain.

The mirror becomes very dark. I wait to see what it will show me next.

Black students march peacefully in the street. Their signs call for an end to segregation. White policemen threaten

the demonstrators with batons, fire hoses, and snarling, snapping dogs. Students are knocked to the ground and thrown against walls by the furious blasts of water. The dogs tear at their limbs. They are arrested and packed into jail. But the students do not fight back. They know that justice is on *their* side.

The scene shifts and I see a young woman sitting at a lunch counter. She is patiently waiting to be served. The white waitress behind the counter sneers and says, "We don't serve your kind here."

Young white men surround the young woman. They call her terrible names and tell her to go home. She does not respond to their insults. Instead, she calmly tells the waitress she is ready to order. The waitress ignores the young woman. Someone pours a glass of milk over her head. Then a bowl of sugar. White patrons in the restaurant howl with laughter.

The young woman looks at me. Though they are trying to humiliate her, they have not touched her soul. She holds her head up and keeps her eyes on the prize.

The mirror grows fuzzy and then clears once more. I hear a chorus of voices shout:

"Say it loud: I'M BLACK AND I'M PROUD!"

Young Black women and men stand shoulder to shoulder, their fists raised defiantly against the sky. All wear black leather jackets, black berets, and black sunglasses. Some of them shoulder guns. They are tired of being patient. They are tired of turning the other cheek. They want Black Power—NOW!

The mirror changes to another scene. A young woman with an Afro stands behind a long table covered with food. She is wearing bell-bottom jeans and a colorful dashiki. A necklace made of cowry shells circles her neck. A button with a prowling black panther is pinned to her shirt.

Children are lined up before her with trays in their hands. She hands each of them a carton of milk, a peanut butter and jelly sandwich, and an orange. The children hurry to an empty seat and devour their food. I can tell that they are hungry.

After breakfast, the children sit in a circle and listen to the young woman. She teaches them about the great

empires of Africa. She points to a map on the wall and shows the children where their ancestors came from. As the children learn about their history, they begin to feel full inside. Though they are poor, they now understand that they have a rich past.

The young woman stands up and goes over to the wall. She turns and looks at me before writing BLACK IS BEAUTIFUL across the board. I smile at her and know that this is true.

The image in the mirror grows dark. I wonder what I will see next…

It's Gramma! She looks much younger than she is now. She walks without a cane, there are no wrinkles around her eyes, and her hair is black instead of gray. At first, I am so excited I do not realize that my grandmother is crying. A handsome man has his arm around her and his eyes are shining, too.

Though he died before I was born, I have seen enough photographs to know that this man is my grandfather.

Gramma takes a handkerchief from her purse and dabs at her eyes. I want to reach through the mirror and give her a hug, but I know I can't.

Gramma and Grandad sit down. Gramma sighs and takes Grandad's hand. "I never thought this day would come," she says.

Grandad squeezes her hand. Then he holds up a camera and gets ready to take a picture.

A man on stage is standing before a microphone. He is wearing a long red and black robe, and a funny velvet hat. He is calling out names. Grandad waits until the man says, "LORETTA HESTON!"

That's my mama!

Grandad stands up and takes a picture as Mama proudly walks across the stage. She is wearing a shiny, purple robe and a square, black hat with a tassel. A sash made of kente cloth is wrapped around her neck. Mama shakes hands with the man before accepting her degree. Then she turns to face Gramma and Grandad. Mama smiles and waves. Grandad takes another picture. Gramma weeps silently.

Afterwards Mama, Gramma, and Grandad hug each

other for a long, long time. Mama's so happy that she can't stop smiling. Gramma and Grandad are too full of pride to speak. Mama is the first person in our family to graduate from college.

When she sees me watching her, Mama smiles even more. One day I will go to college, too. I will make everyone in my family proud of me.

The mirror grows dark again. I wonder how long I have been in the guest room. Outside, the sky is starting to clear. A soft breeze blows through the open window. The sun peeks through the clouds and fills the room with warm sunlight.

I look in the mirror once more but all I see is my own reflection. I look at my lips, my eyes, my nose, and my hair. I touch my cheek, and this time I know that the mean things Malik said are *not* true. I stare at my reflection and see traces of the brave and beautiful women from my past. I know that their pride, courage, and determination are still alive in me.

I lean forward and give myself a kiss. My reflection smiles back at me. I throw the sheet over the magic mirror and head downstairs.

Gramma and Mama are waiting for me in the kitchen.

"Well, baby girl," says Gramma, "how do you feel *now*?"

I wrap my arms around my grandmother and give her a long, strong hug. "I feel *much* better, Gramma," I say.

My grandmother smiles at me and I smile back. I wonder if Mama knows about the magic mirror upstairs. I look at her and Mama winks at me.

"Is anybody hungry?" she asks.

We sit down at the kitchen table. Gramma asks me to say grace.

I thank God for my mother, my grandmother, and for the food we are about to eat. Then I remember the remarkable women in the magic mirror.

I say, "And thank you, Lord, for all the people, past and present, who help me to feel whole in my soul."

Gramma says, "Amen!"

The End

About The Author

Born in Canada, Zetta Elliott moved to the US in 1994. Her books for young readers include the award-winning picture book *Bird*, *A Wish After Midnight*, *Ship of Souls,* and *The Deep*. She lives in Brooklyn and likes birds, glitter, and other magical things.

Learn more at www.zettaelliott.com

About the Illustrator

Paul Melecky developed his love of art at an early age, training in European art schools. He has over 40 years of experience in art design and industrial design, but it was not until he devoted his energy full time to art that he felt free to discover his own artistic voice.

Learn more at www.melecky.com

14745748R10023

Made in the USA
San Bernardino, CA
04 September 2014

Emma Watson

By Petrice Custance

CRABTREE
Publishing Company
www.crabtreebooks.com

CRABTREE
PUBLISHING COMPANY
WWW.CRABTREEBOOKS.COM

Dedicated by Petrice Custance
In memory of an exceptional woman, my grandma, Sally LeBlanc

Author: Petrice Custance

Editor: Ellen Rodger

Proofreader: Lorna Notsch

Photo research: Crystal Sikkens, Ken Wright

Design, and prepress: Ken Wright

Print coordinator: Katherine Berti

Photo Credits

Alamy: title page, London Entertainment; p 4, Allstar Picture Library; p 5, MRP; p 8 (left), LH Images; p 11, PA Images; p 12, Entertainment Pictures; p 14, Allstar Picture Library; p 16, RGR Collection; p 17, EDB Image Archive; p 22 top right), Photo 12; p 23, AF archive; p 26, Europa Newswire; p 27, PACIFIC PRESS; p 28, Geisler-Fotopress

AP Images: p 18, Steven Senne

Getty: p 6, E. Charbonneau; p 7 (top right), Tim Whitby; p 9, AFP Contributor; p 13 (left), UK Press; p 13 (right), William Conran - PA Images; p 15, Dave Hogan; p 20, Dimitrios Kambouris

Keystone: front cover, Armando Gallo; p 22 (bottom), © Summit Entertainment; p 25, © Walt Disney Pictures

Shutterstock: pp 7 (bottom), 8 (right), 10, Featureflash Photo Agency; p 14, Joe Seer; p 21, Sam Aronov; p 24, Sarunyu L

Library and Archives Canada Cataloguing in Publication

Custance, Petrice, author
    Emma Watson / Petrice Custance.

(Superstars!)
Includes index.
Issued in print and electronic formats.
ISBN 978-0-7787-4834-2 (hardcover).--
ISBN 978-0-7787-4860-1 (softcover).--
ISBN 978-1-4271-2097-7 (HTML)

    1. Watson, Emma, 1990- --Juvenile literature. 2. Motion picture actors and actresses--Great Britain--Biography--Juvenile literature. I. Title. II. Series: Superstars! (St. Catharines, Ont.)

PN2598.W38C87 2018   j791.4302'8092   C2018-900281-6
                                          C2018-900282-4

Library of Congress Cataloging-in-Publication Data

CIP available at the Library of Congress

Crabtree Publishing Company
www.crabtreebooks.com   1-800-387-7650

Printed in the U.S.A./052018/BG20180327

Published in Canada
Crabtree Publishing
616 Welland Ave.
St. Catharines, ON
L2M 5V6

Published in the United States
Crabtree Publishing
PMB 59051
350 Fifth Avenue, 59th Floor
New York, New York 10118

Published in the United Kingdom
Crabtree Publishing
Maritime House
Basin Road North, Hove
BN41 1WR

Published in Australia
Crabtree Publishing
3 Charles Street
Coburg North
VIC 3058

CONTENTS

Words that are defined in the glossary are in
bold type the first time they appear in the text.

A Star in the Making

On August 23, 2000, when she was 10 years old, Emma Watson's life changed forever. Emma, Daniel Radcliffe, and Rupert Grint sat in front of more than 50 journalists in London, England, as they were introduced to the world as the stars of the highly anticipated first *Harry Potter* film. Emma needed cushions added to her seat in order to reach the microphone. She later admitted to being terrified when she walked into the room and saw all the flashing cameras, but no one would have guessed. She answered all of the journalists' questions clearly and confidently. By the end of the **press conference**, Emma and her costars had become three of the most famous people on the planet.

Emma has grown up in front of the world's media.

She Said It

"I'm afraid I'm really going to bore you all, but I'm going to stick it in a bank until I'm 21."
—Emma on her first paycheck, at the first *Harry Potter* press conference, August 23, 2000

4

A Mind of Her Own

Emma Watson has not followed the typical path of an international superstar. She has made millions of dollars for movie roles and dabbled in the fashion world, but higher education became her main focus after the *Harry Potter* films came to an end. Today, the work she is most passionate about is her role as an **ambassador** for **UN Women**, her advancement of girls' education, and her involvement in HeForShe. HeForShe is a campaign that invites men and boys to join in the conversation and work toward **gender equality**. As she appears less frequently on the big screen, and devotes more of her time to working for women's rights, Emma is proving herself an admirable role model for young women around the world.

Emma at the ELLE Style Awards in 2014

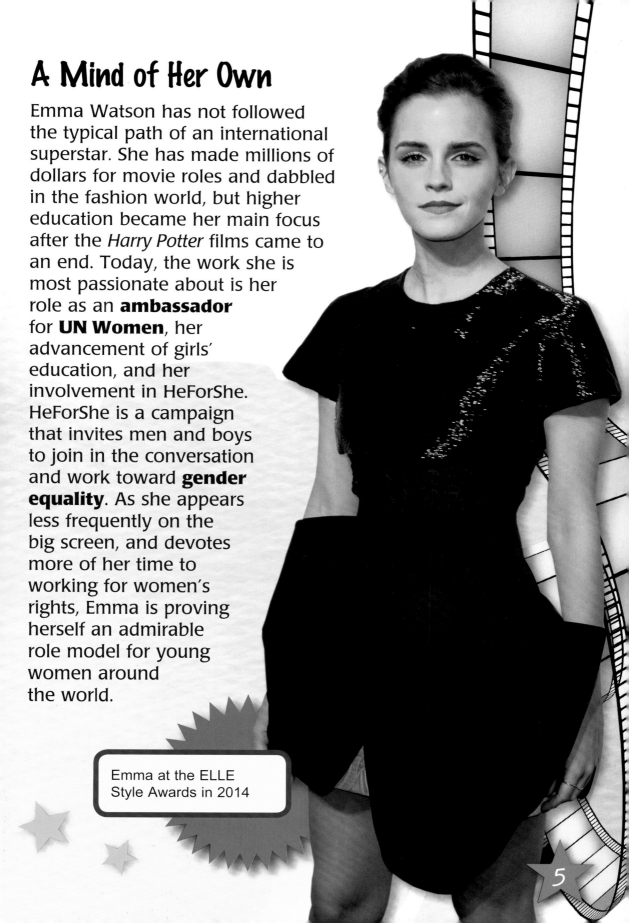

A Star Is Born

Emma Charlotte Duerre Watson was born in Paris, France, on April 15, 1990. Her parents met at Oxford University, in England. After both became lawyers, Emma's parents decided to move to France, where Emma's mother has family. Emma's little brother Alex was born in 1992, and the family lived in Paris until she was five, when her parents separated. Emma has described her parents' divorce as friendly, and she is close with both her mother and father. They have both since remarried, and Emma now has six younger brothers and sisters. Even after many years, Emma says Paris still feels like home to her.

Bonjour

Emma speaks some French, but not nearly as well as she did when living in Paris as a child. She is now working toward becoming **fluent**.

Emma and her family at the 2007 **premiere** of *Harry Potter and the Order of the Phoenix* in Hollywood, California.

Star Light, Star Bright

In 1995, Emma, her mother, and little brother Alex moved from Paris to Oxford, England, while her father moved to London, just over an hour away. She and her brother lived with their mother during the week and traveled to London to see their father every other weekend. Emma has described this living situation as sometimes hectic and stressful.

In 1996, Emma experienced the thrill of her life. Her father took her to London's Oxford Street to watch The Spice Girls, the British band famous for their message of girl power, switch on the street's Christmas lights. Emma had no way of knowing that, eight years later, she would be representing girl power and switching on those same lights!

Emma at the Oxford Street Christmas show in 2004

The Spice Girls were the biggest-selling female group of all time.

The Dream Begins

In 1995, Emma began attending Lynams, a school where students are encouraged to recite poetry and perform in school productions. At age seven, she won a school prize for reciting the poem *The Sea* by James Reeves. The idea of becoming an actress began to take hold in young Emma, and she describes herself as becoming obsessed by the idea. She started appearing in many school plays, and studying at the Oxford branch of Stagecoach Theatre Arts School. There she studied acting, singing, and dancing.

These Stagecoach students are attending a themed tea party.

American Idols

Emma lists Sandra Bullock (right), Julia Roberts, and Goldie Hawn as her earliest acting idols.

Harry Who?

One night before bedtime, Emma's father began reading her and Alex a new book by author J.K. Rowling. The book was called *Harry Potter and the Philosopher's Stone*. (In the United States, it was titled *Harry Potter and the Sorcerer's Stone*.) Emma was quickly enthralled by the story of a young wizard named Harry and his friends, Hermione and Ron. In 1999, when Emma was halfway through *Harry Potter and the Prisoner of Azkaban*, the third book in the series (which she has called her favorite), it was announced that auditions would begin for the first movie of the series.

The *Harry Potter* books are the best-selling book series in history.

She Said It

"I practiced speeches in front of mirrors. Whenever there was a part at school, I went for it. I was probably a bit of a show-off in the sense that, any chance to get up and be seen, I did it."

—Emma on her passion for acting during her schooldays, in *The Telegraph*, December 16, 2007

The Magic Years

Producers for the first *Harry Potter* film searched all over England for the perfect cast. They even searched in schools, including Emma's. Her teachers were asked to recommend 20 children between the ages of nine and 12 to audition. Emma was recommended. David Heyman, one of the film's producers, later said he was impressed with Emma early on, describing her as "astonishingly bright, radiant, and relaxed." The auditions involved the producers asking the actors questions about themselves. They knew whoever they cast would suddenly experience a great deal of attention and fame. The producers wanted to make sure the young actors they chose would be able to deal with such pressure. In the end, Emma went through nine auditions.

Emma's self-confidence helped her win the role and deal with the pressures of playing a beloved character.

Practice Makes Perfect

Emma felt she was meant to play Hermione. She rehearsed constantly, filming herself and then watching to spot where she needed to improve. Emma's parents became worried about the **intensity** of her determination. They didn't want her to be disappointed if she didn't get the role. In the end though, they didn't need to worry. After months of auditions, Emma and Rupert Grint were told together that they had won the roles of Hermione Granger and Ron Weasley. Emma was ecstatic. J.K. Rowling even called to congratulate her. Rowling has said about Emma, "I knew she was perfect from that first phone call." The role is close to Rowling's heart because Hermione is very similar to what she herself was like as a child.

Rupert Grint, author J.K. Rowling, Daniel Radcliffe, and Emma at an appearance for the first film

"" She Said It ""

"I loved the books. I was a massive fan. I just felt like that part belonged to me. I know that sounds crazy, but from that first audition I always knew."
—Emma on her certainty that the role of Hermione would be hers, in *The Telegraph*, April 23, 2009

Learning on the Job

Filming began September 29, 2000, at Leavesden Studios in Hertfordshire, England. Daniel had acted in a few films already, but Rupert and Emma had not. In the early days of filming, their inexperience showed. Rupert had a habit of laughing during his scenes, so the camera had to cut away from him to hide his uncontrollable giggling. Emma's determination to be perfect as Hermione led her to memorize not only her own lines but also everyone else's. She would visibly mouth the words as the other actors were speaking, ruining several takes. These early mistakes were soon corrected though, and the rest of the filming went smoothly.

The three actors on set

Emma, Rupert, and Daniel quickly became friends. In between filming, they played games or rode bikes throughout the massive studio. They spent three to five hours every day studying with onset tutors. Emma loved the schoolwork, but Daniel and Rupert were not as thrilled—just like their *Harry Potter* characters! There were also several onset pranks, including a remote-controlled whoopee cushion (by Daniel) and notes pinned on backs saying "kick me" (by Emma)!

The Magic Is Released

Harry Potter and the Philosopher's Stone had its premiere on November 4, 2001, in London, England. Emma walked the red carpet with her brother Alex. She revealed to one reporter, "I'm so nervous I feel like I'm going to be sick." The film was a massive worldwide success. Emma received many positive reviews for her portrayal of Hermione. One critic called her performance "sassy and smart."

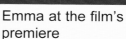

Emma at the film's premiere

" She Said It "

"I just remember the wide-eyed excitement and awe. I just came into Leavesden every day, just to be so excited about what I was going to see next. Every time I walked on to a new set or someone new did something new, it was all just so overwhelmingly exciting. It just went by like this [snaps fingers] doing that movie."
—Emma on her memory of filming the first *Harry Potter* film, on ComingSoon.net, November 15, 2010

The Glare of the Spotlight

Now that Emma was an international superstar, her mother gave her some important advice. She told Emma to keep the friends she already had, because she would never have to wonder if they liked her for herself or for her fame. Her mother's wisdom helped Emma stay level-headed. Over the next 10 years, she starred in seven more *Harry Potter* films. Growing up in the eye of the media, Emma became skilled at handling questions from journalists, which could sometimes be rude and **intrusive**. She was often asked if she had a crush on any of her costars. Emma would patiently explain that her relationships with Daniel and Ron were more like brother and sister. She described Daniel as the person she could go to if she needed to talk, and Rupert as someone to eat candy with and have fun.

Em-Crush

Emma has long had a crush on the actor Kevin Costner!

Emma at the premiere of *Harry Potter and the Chamber of Secrets*

Growing Pains

As the three actors headed into adolescence, a time when most young people deal with feelings of uncertainty and self-consciousness, it was difficult to have the media and people around the world **scrutinizing** them. An example of this happened during the filming of *Harry Potter and the Chamber of Secrets*. Hermione was supposed to run down a hall to Harry and hug him. The thought of doing this flustered Emma. There were 350 other actors on set to witness it. Take after take, Emma would give Daniel a quick embrace and then run away and hide. The director had to piece different shots together during editing, to make the hug look believable.

Shy Guy

Emma wasn't the only one to be embarrassed by emotional scenes. On the prospect of filming Ron's growing feelings for Hermione, Rupert Grint once said, "I hope it doesn't happen. I hope Ron gets killed off before they actually do something."

Grin and Bear It

The last book of the *Harry Potter* series was divided into two movies—*Harry Potter and the Deathly Hallows* Parts 1 and 2. The movies were shot back-to-back, between February 2009 and the summer of 2010. It was a difficult shoot for Emma because she had to spend long periods soaking wet, after she and Ron get dropped into a freezing cold lake by a dragon!

What Rupert had dreaded a few years earlier was finally about to happen—he and Emma would share an onscreen kiss. In fact, Hermione also had to share a kiss with Harry. Despite their squeamishness—and much giggling—Emma and her two costars managed to act professionally and get the job done.

Free Stuff

After filming, Emma got to keep Hermione's time turner, cloak, and wand. She cherishes these reminders of her happy *Harry Potter* years.

Saying Good-bye

On the very last day of filming, cast and crew watched a video of behind-the-scenes moments from the entire series. Emma was the first to break down in tears. Her years on *Harry Potter* sets, from ages 10 to 20, had provided some consistency in her life, in contrast to the hectic shuttling between her parents' homes and then the addition of many new siblings. Her costars, producers, crew, and her driver, Nigel, had been like family to her. Although Emma was very excited for the next chapter in her life, she was also struggling with the reality of saying good-bye to Hermione, who had given Emma so much and completely changed her life.

By the end of the movie series, Emma was walking the red carpet and handling the press like a pro.

66 She Said It 99

"I feel like someone's dying. I know that sounds like an exaggeration but I really do. Everything is so linked to my life and growing up…I'm just so unbelievably proud to have been part of this. I feel like the luckiest girl in the world."

—Emma on how she felt near the end of the *Harry Potter* films, from *Emma Watson: The Biography*

Life after Hermione

Education has always been very important to Emma. Her parents supported her and hoped she would stay in England to attend Cambridge University. Emma, showing her characteristic independence, decided to move an ocean away. In the fall of 2009, she began studying at Brown, an **Ivy League** university in Providence, Rhode Island. Unfortunately, Emma's first day at Brown did not go smoothly. A fake story online claimed she had arrived on campus by helicopter, and many people believed it. Emma's representatives were concerned that she was being portrayed as a spoiled celebrity and issued a denial. Then, paparazzi were able to get shots of her on campus during orientation activities, which raised concerns about campus safety. Fellow students were also approaching Emma asking for autographs. Emma just wanted to be a normal student and experience university life like anyone else.

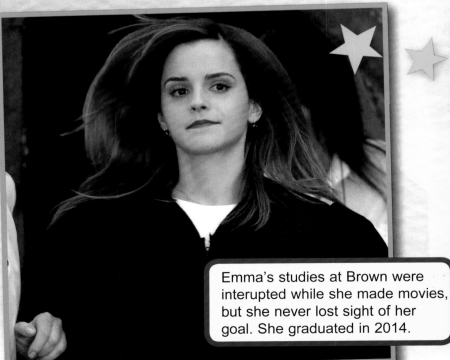

Emma's studies at Brown were interupted while she made movies, but she never lost sight of her goal. She graduated in 2014.

18

We're Not at Hogwarts Anymore

On one occasion in a lecture hall, Emma quickly held up her hand to answer a professor's question in a style very similar to Hermione. Someone yelled out, "Ten points for Gryffindor!" However, after the initial interest, Emma's fellow Brown students began to accept her as just another student. She lived in a dorm and shared a bathroom with seven other people. She often walked down the hall to her room with her wet hair in a towel, and not a single person posted an image of her on social media. She made several friends, took part in dramatic productions on campus, attended football games, and played field hockey. Emma has said that, after a bumpy start, her years at Brown were extremely happy. She graduated with a degree in English literature in 2014.

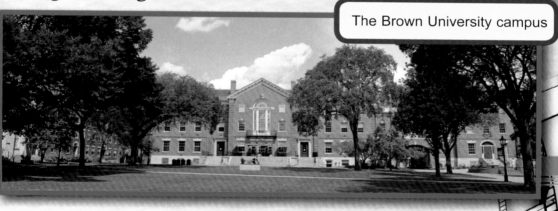

The Brown University campus

He Said It

"Emma is astonishingly bright and just anxious to move forward with life. She's been amazing to watch. She has these choices. She could be an actress or a model, but with her studies and success she could also be a lawyer. She could also be an artist....It's pretty amazing to see."
—Producer David Heyman on Emma in the *L.A. Times*, July 2, 2009

Style and Kindness

Ever since she walked her first red carpet in 2001, Emma has been a fashion icon. Her style has changed often over the years, and she now has a **stylist** to help her make an impact when doing press events. Emma has also modeled for beauty and fashion brands Lancôme and Burberry, even appearing in ads with her brother, Alex.

Her main fashion focus now is **sustainable** clothing. In 2009, she helped design a line of **eco-friendly** clothes with the fashion label People Tree. In 2016, Emma attended the Met Gala, a major event held every year in New York. She wore a gown made from recycled plastic bottles. In February 2017, Emma launched a new Instagram account called The Press Tour to promote the sustainable fashions and cosmetics that she wears.

Clothes

One of Emma's reasons for wearing eco-friendly clothing is the fact that the fashion industry is the second-biggest polluter of fresh water on the planet.

Short and Sweet

While much of the attention on Emma's appearance has been positive, some of it has not. On August 5, 2010, Emma posted a picture of herself with a new, short haircut. The response was intense. There was a lot of debate about why she would chop her beautiful locks, which had been Hermione's defining feature. Emma's contract had not allowed her to cut her hair during the 10 years of filming. By cutting her hair in 2010, Emma was signaling to the world that she was starting a new adult phase of her life, and she was free to make decisions for herself.

" She Said It "

"The moment I cut my hair I felt I became a woman. Now I'm ready to start taking risks."
—Emma in *The Mirror*, November 16, 2010

Hermione Who?

Emma had been worried that she would be **typecast** as an actor after playing Hermione for so long, but her film career in the years following the *Harry Potter* films has been varied and well received by critics.

Emma's first film after *Harry Potter* was a small role in the critically acclaimed *My Week with Marilyn*. Set in the 1950s, she plays Lucy, a wardrobe assistant on the set of a movie starring Marilyn Monroe. One reviewer said Emma was being "underused," while another referred to her as a "sweet, likeable, very British alternative to Monroe."

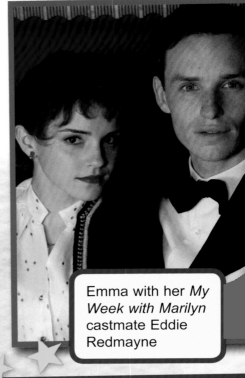

Emma with her *My Week with Marilyn* castmate Eddie Redmayne

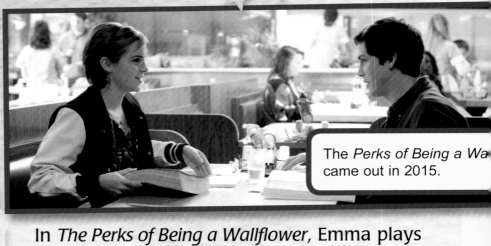

The *Perks of Being a Wa* came out in 2015.

In *The Perks of Being a Wallflower*, Emma plays Sam, a kind but insecure American teenager. Shot in only six weeks, and mostly at night, Emma has said it was the most exhausting shoot she's ever experienced.

The Bling Ring, which came out in 2013, is based on the true story of a group of friends who robbed the homes of celebrities in Los Angeles in 2008 and 2009. Emma plays Nicki, a character based on one of the robbers, who is obsessed with celebrities and fame. During filming, Emma watched videos of Kim Kardashian to try to pick up her accent, as she thought it would be perfect for the role of Nicki. Emma's portrayal of the very un-Hermione-like Nicki received much critical praise.

In *The Bling Ring,* Emma liked the challenge of playing someone so unlike herself.

Living the Dream, One Heist at a Time

THE BLING RING

Written and Directed by SOFIA COPPOLA
Based on Actual Events

A24

She Said It

"I'm probably the least obvious choice to play the role, as she's the epitome of everything that I am considered not to be. We're polar opposites. When I read the script and I realized that essentially it was a **meditation** *on fame and what it's become to our society, I had to do it."* —Emma on her reasons for wanting to portray Nicki in *The Bling Ring,* in *British GQ,* May 3, 2013

Girl Power

On January 26, 2015, Emma announced that she would be starring as another heroine from her childhood—Belle from *Beauty and the Beast*. Before shooting for the live-action film began, Emma attended a "princess boot camp" to prepare for the role. The intensive three-month training included singing, dancing, and riding lessons. Dan Stevens, the actor playing the Beast, shot many of his scenes with Emma wearing stilts! This was to help give her an idea of the height his character would be in the finished film, with the help of **computer animation**.

Rebel Princess

Emma actually had the chance to be a different Disney princess. She was offered the role of Cinderella for the 2015 film version. She turned it down because she didn't feel a connection to the character. Belle, however, was a different story. Emma believes Belle is an excellent role model for young girls because she thinks for herself and takes an active role in deciding her own destiny. Emma helped design Belle's everyday dress, with pockets for books and tools, and she insisted that Belle wear sturdy, practical boots, not dainty slippers. She has referred to Belle as "a rebellious Disney princess." Emma has said that, through Belle's love of books, one of the best messages *Beauty and the Beast* inspires is the importance of education. Access to education for girls around the world is a cause that Emma has increasingly dedicated herself to.

She Said It

"I think that I just feel really lucky. For me, Belle was my childhood heroine; [the film] came out two days after I was born. And then, in my early teens, it was about idolizing Hermione. So to be given the chance to play my two childhood idols is probably a very unique and rare experience for an actress."
—Emma in the *Irish Independent*, March 19, 2017

Shining a Light

In July 2014, Emma was appointed an ambassador for UN Women. In this role, she works to promote gender equality and improve education for girls around the world—an issue she is passionate about. In 2016, Emma traveled to Malawi in Africa to help shine a global spotlight on the need to end child marriage and keep young girls in school. Emma refers to herself as a gender equality **activist** and says she is committed to helping build the **feminist** movement into an "unstoppable current."

School's Out

It is estimated that worldwide, 51 million girls are child brides, meaning they were married before the age of 18. Many of those girls have been forced to quit school.

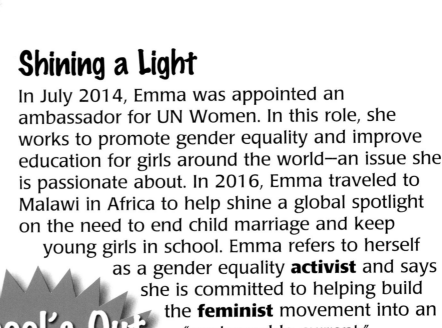

EMMA WATSON

SECRETARY-GENERAL

Hear Her Roar

On September 20, 2014, Emma wrote and delivered an electrifying speech before the United Nations. She announced the launch of HeForShe, an organization that calls for boys and men to participate in the fight for gender equality. In her speech, Emma discussed the importance of feminism, and she argued that harmful **stereotypes** of what it means to be a boy or man must stop. Emma received much positive press coverage for her speech, but she also received some threats. She has stated that those threats only deepened her commitment to working for gender equality.

Emma spoke at the UN Women launch of HeForShe Arts Week on International Women's Day in 2016.

「「She Said It 」」

"I started questioning gender-based assumptions a long time ago. When I was eight, I was confused for being called bossy because I wanted to direct the plays that we would put on for our parents, but the boys were not."—Words from Emma's speech at the United Nations in New York, during the launch of HeForShe, on September 20, 2014

27

Being a Change Maker

An avid reader, Emma launched Our Shared Shelf on Goodreads, a website for people to share book recommendations. Our Shared Shelf is a book club that encourages people around the

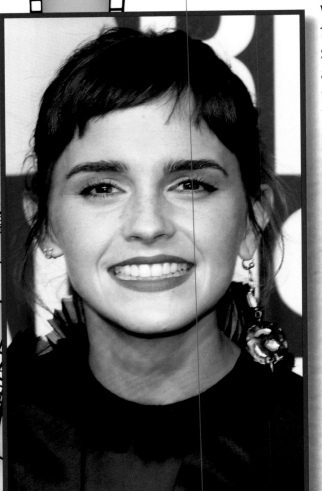

world to learn more about feminism. She has been spotted in New York, London, and Paris working as a "book ninja," leaving free copies of books in public places for people to discover and read.

Emma last appeared in the movie *The Circle* with Tom Hanks in April 2017. She also announced she was taking time off from acting to devote herself to her work for gender equality. She proudly wore black to the 75th Golden Globe Awards in support of the Time's Up campaign, which seeks to end gender-based **harassment** and discrimination.

❝ She Said It ❞

"I'm reading a lot this year, and I want to do a lot of listening...I want to listen to as many different women in the world as I can."
—Emma on her gender equality work, in *PAPER* magazine, February 18, 2016

Timeline

1990: Emma is born in Paris, France, on April 15

1995: Moves with her mother and brother to Oxford, England

1997: First reads the book *Harry Potter and the Philosopher's Stone*

1999: Auditions for *Harry Potter* film

2000: Introduced to the world as the actress who will play Hermione Granger at her first press conference on August 23. Filming begins at Leavesden Studios on September 29.

2001: Walks her first red carpet for the premiere of *Harry Potter and the Philosopher's Stone*

2009: Begins studies at Brown University

2009: Designs an eco-friendly line of clothing for People Tree

2011: *Harry Potter and the Deathly Hallows* Part 2, the final film in the series, premieres

2014: Graduates from Brown University

2014: Becomes ambassador for UN Women. Delivers powerful speech to UN at launch of HeForShe.

2016: Launches Our Shared Shelf on Goodreads.

2016: Attends the Met Gala in New York City wearing a dress made of recycled bottles

2017: Stars as Belle in *Beauty and the Beast*

2018: Wears black at 75th Golden Globe Awards to spotlight gender-based harassment and discrimination

Glossary

activist A person who works to create political or social change

ambassador A representative or supporter of a specific group

computer animation The use of computer programs to create moving images onscreen

eco-friendly Not harmful to the environment

feminist A person who believes in equal treatment and opportunity for men and women

fluent Able to speak smoothly without pausing

gender equality Equal rights for all genders

harassment Pressuring or agressively bothering

intensity Having or showing strong feelings or opinions

intrusive Inappropriately curious

Ivy League A group of schools in the United States with a reputation for academic excellence

meditation Careful focus or thought

premiere The first performance of a musical or theatrical work

press conference A meeting to provide journalists with information to be reported in the news media

producer A person responsible for the financing and overall management of a production, such as a movie

scrutinize To examine closely

stereotype A widely held but oversimplified view of something or someone

sustainable Does not deplete natural resources

stylist A person who advises others on fashion

typecast When an actor is continuously given the same kind of role

UN Women An United Nations organization working for gender equality around the world

Find Out More

Books

Baker, Felicity. *Hermione Granger: Cinematic Guide.* Scholastic, 2016.

Higgins, Nadia. *Emma Watson: From Wizards to Wallflowers.* Lerner Classroom, 2014.

Nolan, David. *Emma Watson: The Biography.* John Blake, 2011.

Websites

HeForShe
www.heforshe.org

Our Shared Shelf
www.goodreads.com/group/show/179584-our-shared-shelf

The Press Tour
www.instagram.com/the_press_tour

UN Women
www.unwomen.org

Index

About the Author

Petrice Custance is a writer and editor. She is happiest when she is walking her dogs, Bickey and Mickey, or getting pelted with snowballs by her nephews, Kyle and Tyler.